I0712796

HOLEY MOLEY

AND THE QUEST FOR THE GOLDEN GLASSES

BY TREY CALLAHAN

ADVENTURE AWAITS!

Holey Moley was a mole,
But he did not live in a hole.
He lived in Moland, on an island far away.
It was a mining town, and it was all gray.

There was nothing to do, nothing but work.
And if you did not, the others would smirk.

The repetition seemed to go on forever.

He would daydream sometimes but then he would remember

That life would not change on this island called Moland,

Where everyone worked and mined in the sand.

Then one day an opportunity came

In the form of an empty box—a pain!

Holey Moley was out of contacts, oh no!

Without them he could not see past his nose.

So, he went to the store but was met with surprise…
The shelves were empty! There were no more supplies!

This worried mole went to talk to a friend

Who usually helped his troubles to end.

His friend had an idea that would shock the masses:

"The golden glasses? What ever are those? "

"They will help you to see past your nose!

They are magical glasses and if they are found

The rodent that wears them will see all around!

Without help from contacts, you will see!

I'm sure if you find them your troubles will ease!"

"That sounds great!" Said Holey with glee.

"Where do I go? And what help should I seek?"

"You should seek help from your neighbors and friends,

Because without them you may never find an end

To the journey," said the mole with answers to the questions,

"And they might teach you some valuable lessons!"

"That's great advice!" Holey Moley said quickly.

And he dashed away lickety-split-ly

To gather a group of moles to join his team

To find the glasses with a golden gleam.

Holey knocked on doors left and right,

But many moles were too uptight

To leave their lives that they lived in the town.

But Holey Moley kept searching up and down.

Finally Holey had gathered a crew

Made up of friends and even a few

Moles that Holey had not met before

Who all faced the problem involving the store.

They gathered some supplies and got ready to depart,

And each mole promised to do their part

And cooperate when times get tough

And be nice to each other, rather than gruff.

The first thing they did was they got aboard

A treasure ship to go and look for a hoard

Of gold and riches, like pirates keep,

Since if there be gold, they may find what they seek.

The captain seemed nice but was a little strict

And he made sure that if they licked

Any food that didn't belong to them,

Then they would walk the plank and swim

Back to old Moland, boring and dark

And hopefully not get eaten by a shark.

The captain's first mate was also demanding—
She made the moles agree to swear while standing
That they would behave and not cause a stir
Or else they'd draw the attention of some others with fur.

The others were a dangerous group made of rats

And they would sink the captain's ship and laugh.

The piRAT crew sent shivers to all.

Holey's friends wanted no trouble, these rats could brawl.

So Holey's team pledged to comply,

And the crew was so happy that they could cry,

Since danger seemed to be unlikely

Aboard this ship sailing the high seas.

It was mostly smooth sailing but then came a twist…

Someone spotted a second ship through the mist!

The sails were all tattered and it had a broken mast,
But even with this the ship was moving fast!

"Such bad luck since we were almost at the treasure,"

Thought the captain, his right hand, and his crew all together.

"Ready your weapons!" came a cry from above

And Holey Moley's team flew like a dove

To their stations which were assigned based on their skill.

They were not going to let the piRATs break their will!

As the ships drew closer, a battle began.

It was quite a racket, like pots hitting pans.

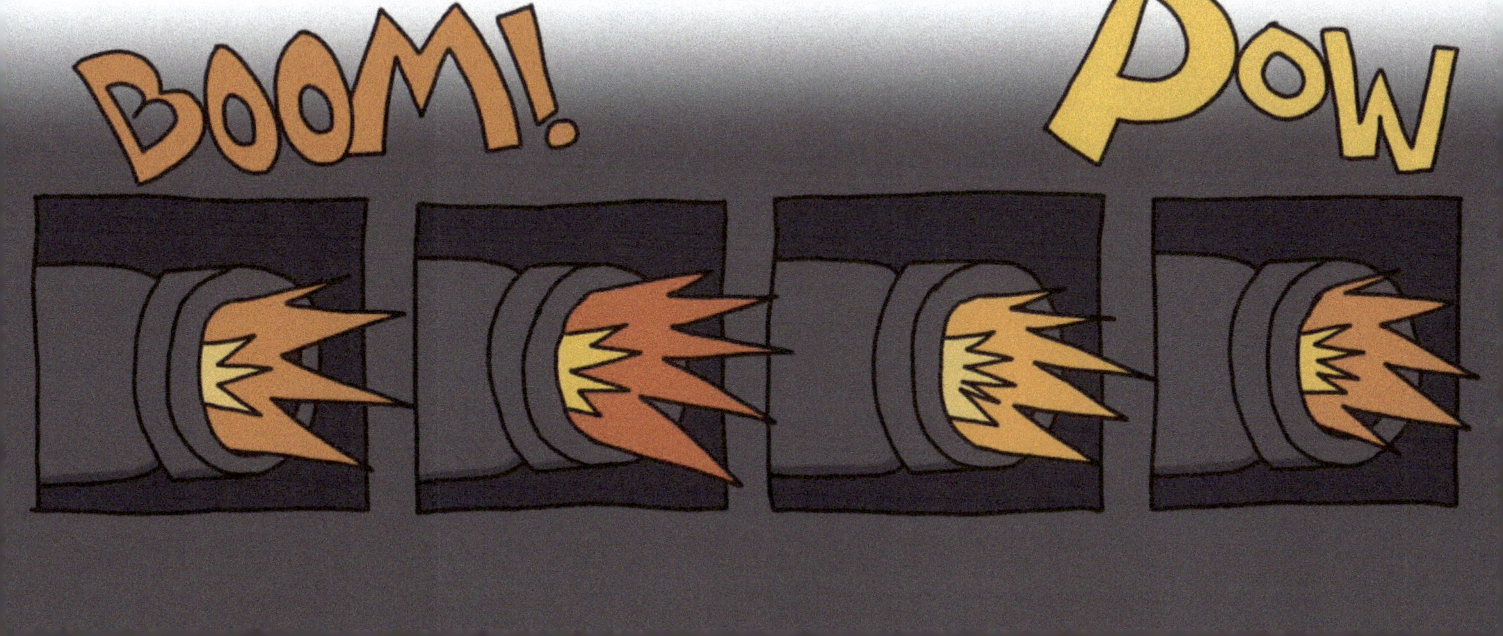

Both sides were using everything they had

To get to that treasure and end the bad

Luck that they met on the ocean wavies,

And also to avoid a meeting in Davy's

Locker down below, you see,

Because no rodent wants to end up with he.

The battle lasted for no more than an hour,

With the rodents on deck using all of their power.

Finally, they sank the piRAT ship

And made sure that they would never grip

The gold they searched for upon the shore.

Those rats would be pirates no more.

Some smooth sailing later, someone called "Land Ho!"
And they docked the ship where the water's shallow.

The whole crew searched their best

And the rodents dug up a treasure chest.

They looked for the golden glasses again and again

But this was not where their journey would end.

So, the crew brought the moles back to land

And the captain gave the team a new errand:

"Maybe search in the buildings of old

Where once stood rodents who were very bold.

The ancient ones shared wisdom here in the form of classes.

Maybe they had worn the golden glasses?"

Holey Moley and his friends agreed
To try this place but first they'd need
A map of how to get there from here.
"Of course!" said the captain "never fear!
For I have a map for that purpose for you!"
And he pulled out a map which was far from new.

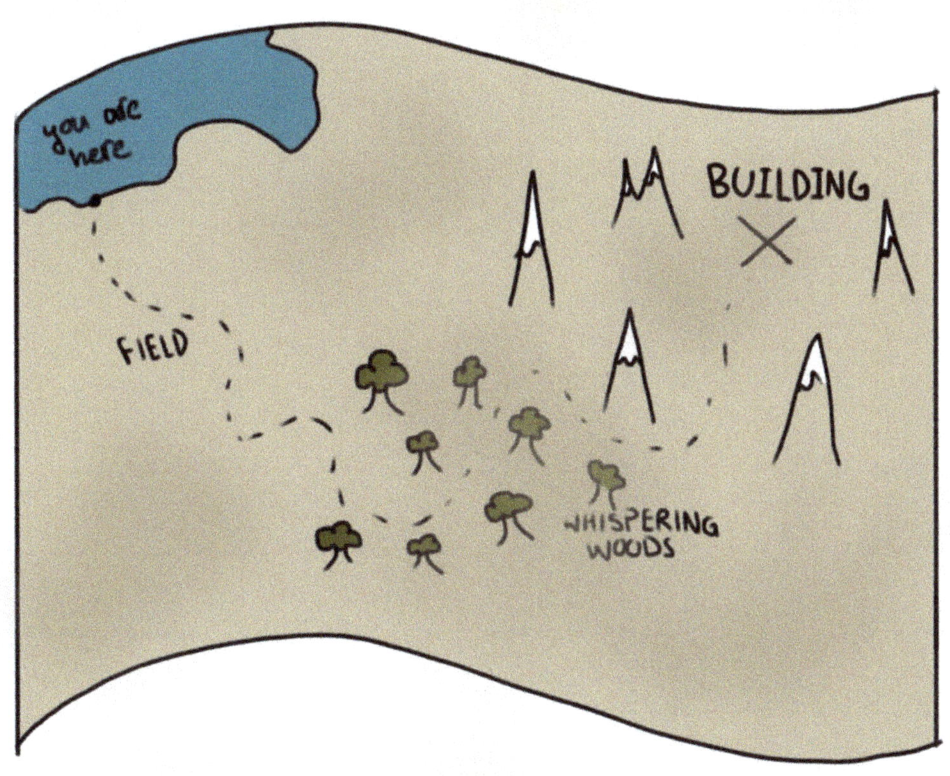

He handed Holey the tattered old map,

Which Holey threw into his trusty sack.

Here started the next part of the voyage.

They waved goodbye and all were joyous.

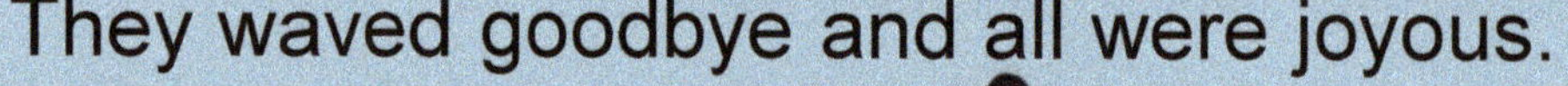

The crew they left with lots of treasure

And the Moles now set off on another adventure.

The first stop on the map was a great big field.

Crossing it would have caused others to yield

Before they found the building of old,

But this team didn't stop, they broke the mold.

The field went on for miles and miles,

With mountains and rivers scattered all the while.

There was rain and wind and blistering heat

Which would make any other moles retreat.

But this would not stop Holey Moley's crew.

They just kept going...wouldn't you?

The second stop was the whispering woods,

Where the trees would talk and make sure you understood.

They would tell scary stories or myths from long ago,

They would tell the moles to go back, but no!

Holey Moley led them through

And soon they saw the sky's bright blue.

They were past the whispering woods at last.

Next up was a huge mountain, so vast.

But the moles were not afraid of a couple of cliffs.

Their mines were far more scary than this!

They got to work and climbed up high

And soon they were way up in the sky,

Above the clouds, above the trees.

At last, the building from the map was what they could see.

They went inside and met with a mouse.

He was old and wise, and this was his house.

He protected the books and the legends inside

and he shared the stories with wonder and pride.

Holey asked "do you know of these?"

And he held up a picture for the mouse to see.

"I know of them, certainly," said the wise old rodent.

"But I don't have any idea where they went!"

"Last I heard they were in a dragon's lair."

"Of course!" said Holey Moley, "Let's go there!"

"But how will we find it?" said one of the moles.

"It's the next mountain over" said the mouse with a scroll.

The scroll contained lots of secrets inside.

It was a generous gift the old mouse supplied.

With that, Holey's crew waved and left

And they continued their journey to see what was next.

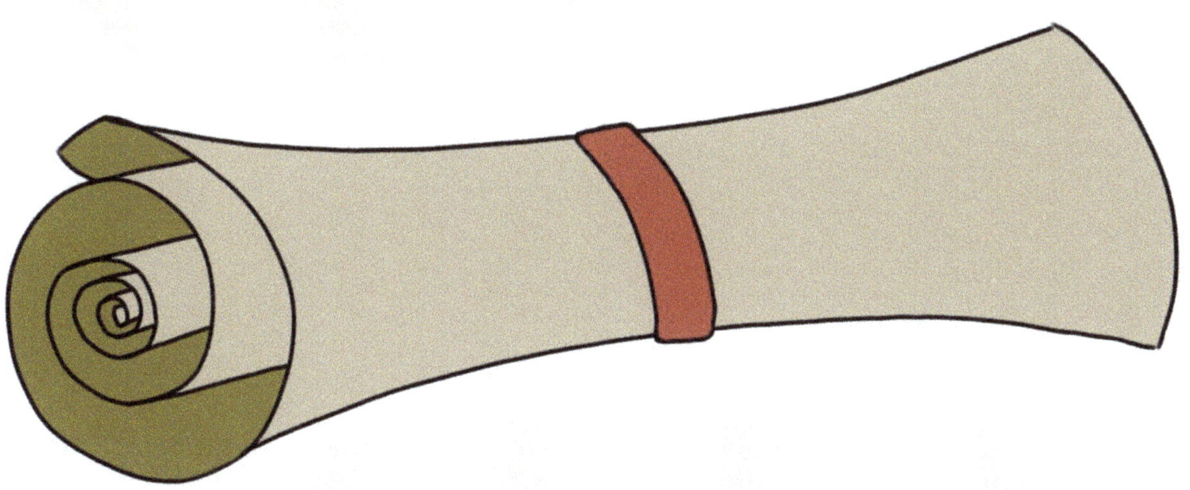

The next mountain was much like the first

Though there was a river which is the absolute worst

Thing to encounter as moles are bad swimmers.

Luckily, they came across some fallen timber.

The log allowed them to cross safely.

Next, they marched up the mountain bravely.

This time, they didn't have to climb as high,

Because halfway up something caught their eye…

Smoke and fire shot out of a crack

And one of the moles screamed out with an ACK!

This must be the lair of the dragon who lived here

And this gave the team a reason to fear,

Because they had never seen a dragon before

But they had heard lots of descriptive lore.

Nevertheless, they continued on

And they went into the hole in the lawn.

What they were met with was a very strange sight...

It was a rat dressed as a dragon! and he was rather polite!

He said, "Hello visitors, how can I help?

I don't get many visits!" and he gave out a yelp.

"You must be on a quest of sorts!

In that case let me put on my questing shorts!"

The rat left and then came back in a hurry.

The shorts he was wearing were bright blue and furry.

"Please feel free to look through my treasure!

And please come back to visit whenever!"

The moles then searched around the room

For the golden glasses, as you may assume.

These glasses were not easily found,
Even after looking all around,
And not even the rat in his questing shorts
Could find the glasses in his great big fort.

"Well, I'm sorry to disappoint," said the rat.

"But I'm so happy to have visitors that

I will help you search elsewhere, too,

If you would let me come with you."

Holey Moley agreed and they went on their way

With no new glasses, but a new friend, yay!

Their next stop was a mystery place,

Because the group had no map to trace.

They walked and walked but they saw no hint

Of how to find the glasses with a golden glint.

They had absolutely no idea where to go.

Then they saw something...A brilliant rainbow!

"The pot of gold!" they exclaimed, "Of course!"

And they took off running like a racehorse.

The rodents were close when, from out of sight,

A group of leprechauns jumped out to fight!

"You can't have our gold!" they shouted,

"Because if you do, we'd have none!" they pouted.

"Without our gold we are nothing" they cried.

"Well, that's not true" Holey Moley replied.

"We just want to look; I want you to know this.

And besides, what you say here is bogus.

You are so much more than your gold.

You are you and that's something to behold."

"Why thank you mole," the lead leprechaun said.

"Well in that case, go right ahead."

So, the rodent team got to looking.

But in all the pots of gold they found nothing

That resembled the golden glasses in mind.

Golden coins were all they could find.

The rodents thanked the leprechauns

And then they wearily continued on.

"I think this is where our journey ends,"
Said Holey Moley to his friends.
And with that one mole said:
"There is one more place to check instead!"

"There is a wizard who lives near Moland.

I wonder if he would lend a hand?"

Holey got excited again.

"Yes, of course! Come with me friends!"

And then they returned, back to Moland

With lots of hope and big plans.

They left the mountains and the rivers,
They left the woods that gave them shivers.

They got aboard a little boat

That promised to keep them afloat.

It was not as grand as the treasure ship,

But it offered safety on their trip.

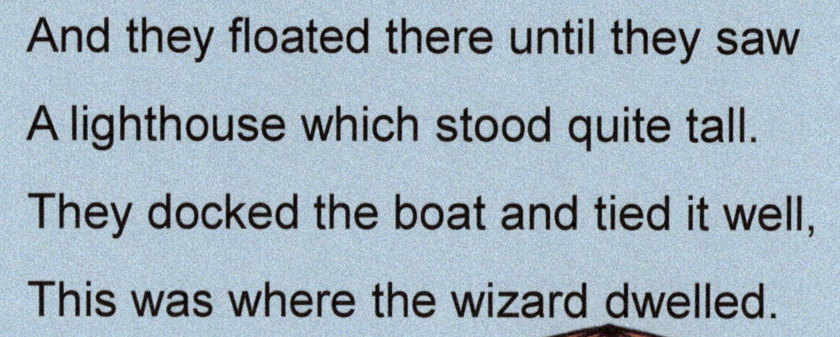

And they floated there until they saw

A lighthouse which stood quite tall.

They docked the boat and tied it well,

This was where the wizard dwelled.

They went to the door with nervous excitement,

Because who knows where this might end?

Holey Moley's hand went knock, knock.

The door swung open and then it stopped.

"Why hello!" the wizard said.

He had the glasses on his head!

THE
END!

ISBN: 979-8-218-91181-2